HALLOWEEN PARADE

Look for these
and other books
in
The Kids in Ms. Colman's Class series

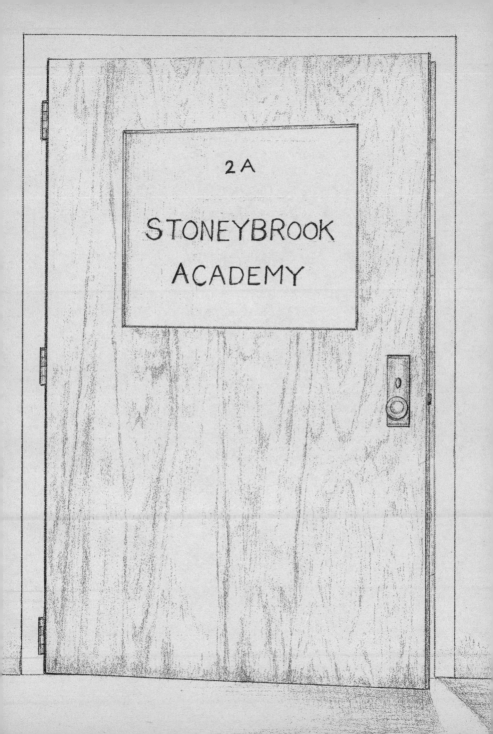

Jannie, Bobby, Tammy, Sara
Ian, Leslie, Hank, Terri
Nancy, Omar, Audrey, Chris, Ms. Colman
Karen, Hannie, Ricky, Natalie

THE KIDS IN
Ms. COLMAN'S CLASS

HALLOWEEN PARADE

Ann M. Martin

Illustrations by Charles Tang

A
LITTLE APPLE
PAPERBACK

SCHOLASTIC INC.
New York Toronto London Auckland Sydney

ISBN 0-590-06001-5

12 11 10 9 8 7 6 5 4 3 2 1   7 8 9/9 0 1 2/0

Printed in the U.S.A.   40
First Scholastic printing, September 1997

*This book is in honor of
the birth of
Rachel Godwin Allen*

GLASSES

Hannie Papadakis sat down at her desk in room 2A, Ms. Colman's classroom. She was one of the first people to arrive at Stoneybrook Academy that Monday morning. Even Ms. Colman had not arrived yet. But the door to Mr. Berger's room was open. Hannie could peer through it and see Mr. Berger next door. He was at his desk. Hannie knew he was keeping an eye on her classroom until Ms. Colman came in.

"Hi, Hannie!" called Terri Barkan as she ran into the room.

"Hi, Hannie!" called Tammy Barkan.

"Hi!" Hannie replied.

Terri and Tammy were twins, which

1

Hannie thought was extremely cool. If they dressed alike, Hannie could not even tell them apart. Ms. Colman did not let them sit next to each other, though. Tammy sat in the second row, and Terri sat in the third.

Hannie sat in the fourth row, which was the back row of the classroom. Her best friend, Karen Brewer, sat in the fourth row too. Hannie did not get to sit *next* to Karen, but that was all right. Nancy Dawes sat between Karen and Hannie, and Nancy (who was Karen's other best friend) was getting to be Hannie's friend too. Hannie wished that one day the three of them could all be best friends, but she had a feeling that might take time. Nancy was still shy around Hannie. And she was a little jealous that Karen was friends with Hannie. Oh well. Hannie could wait. She was a patient person.

Hannie pulled a book out of her desk. She had just begun to read a spooky Halloween story when someone tapped her on the shoulder.

"*Boo!*" yelled the someone.

"Aughh!" Hannie cried loudly. "Karen Brewer, you scared me!"

Karen giggled. "Well, you were reading a Halloween book."

"Hi, you guys!"

"Hi, Nancy," called Hannie and Karen.

Hannie put her book away. Her friends were there. Now the day had truly begun.

Hannie and Nancy and Karen watched the rest of their classmates arrive. First

Ricky Torres joined them in the back row. He could be a pest, so Hannie was glad when he left the girls alone.

Then Omar Harris, Ian Johnson, and Hank Reubens came in. Ricky ran to them, and they made a huddle in the corner.

Jannie Gilbert and Leslie Morris arrived next. They were best friends. And they were the best enemies of Hannie, Nancy, and Karen. Jannie pulled Leslie into the coatroom to show her something she was carrying in her pocket.

Messy Natalie Springer entered the classroom by herself. She pulled up her droopy socks, pushed her glasses up on her nose, and sat down.

Finally Chris Lamar, Bobby Gianelli, Audrey Green, and Sara Ford arrived. Sara dashed to her seat. Hannie was pretty sure she was escaping from Bully Bobby. He was probably up to another one of his mean tricks.

Sara's seat was in front of Hannie's, but before Hannie could ask her about

Bobby, Ms. Colman arrived. She set her things on her desk. And the kids in her class scurried to their seats.

Ms. Colman was Hannie's favorite teacher. In fact, she was just about everyone's favorite teacher. Ms. Colman was kind, she was funny, she thought up great projects and activities. And she almost never yelled.

"Class," said Ms. Colman a few minutes later, "I have an announcement to make. Tomorrow you will all go to the nurse's office to have your vision tested. An eye doctor is going to decide whether any of you might need glasses."

Karen raised her hand. "Oh, Ms. Colman," she said. "I will not need to take the test. I just went to my family's eye doctor, and I already know that I need glasses. I am getting them very soon."

"Okay, Karen. I will check that with your mother this afternoon," said Ms. Colman. "Now, class, please find your reading books."

2

HALLOWEEN

Hannie thought about the vision test during school that day. She thought about it on the way home. She wondered what the test would be like. Would it be hard? She thought about glasses too. Would she need them? What would glasses feel like resting on her nose?

Hannie decided to think about something else. "Mommy? Can Karen come over today?" she asked.

"Sure," replied Mrs. Papadakis. "Give her a call."

Karen lived in another neighborhood. Hannie wished Karen lived closer by so that she could walk to her house. Actually,

every other weekend, Karen did live across the street from Hannie. Karen's parents were divorced, and Karen lived with her father two weekends each month, and with her mother the rest of the time. Her father's house was across the street from Hannie's. Two weekends each month was not very often, though, Hannie thought. Plus, Karen's mother's house was next door to Nancy's. Lucky Nancy. Karen and Nancy got to see each other nearly every day after school. That was why they were best friends. If Hannie lived next door to Nancy, maybe they would be best friends too.

Hannie called Karen. Karen's mother said she could drive Karen to Hannie's house if Mrs. Papadakis could drive her back later. And before Hannie knew it, her doorbell was ringing.

"I'll get it!" cried Hannie's older brother, Linny.

"No, me! No, me!" cried Hannie's baby sister, Sari.

"No, *me*!" said Hannie. "That is Karen. *My* friend. So *I* will answer the door." And she did.

"Let's play outside," said Karen after she had waved good-bye to her mother. "And let's talk about our Halloween costumes."

Karen always had lots of ideas about things to do. Some of the kids in Ms. Colman's class thought she was bossy. And maybe she was a little bossy. But Hannie liked Karen anyway.

"I think I might be a magic genie," said Hannie.

"I might be a witch," said Karen. "But I do not know. I am almost always a witch. I have that tall black hat and that — Hannie? Are you listening to me?"

"What? Oh, sorry. Karen, I just remembered something. The costumes made me think of it."

"Think of what?"

"Well, I was remembering last night when I heard Daddy talking on the phone.

9

He was talking to someone from his office. And I heard him say something like, 'Everything is ordered, and it should be here in time for Halloween. There will be plenty for everyone.' And *then* he said, 'Yes, it is all free.'"

"So?" said Karen.

"Well, where does my father work?" asked Hannie.

"At a company?" replied Karen.

"At a company that makes *costumes*."

"Costumes? I thought it made uniforms. Like for nurses and police officers."

"*And* it makes costumes. And some other stuff. Anyway, Daddy said everything is ordered, there will be plenty for everyone, and it will be here for *Halloween*. That must mean costumes. Daddy probably got a whole bunch of free Halloween costumes this year. I bet he will have enough for every kid in our class. And for every kid in Linny's class."

"Free costumes for everyone?" exclaimed Karen.

Hannie nodded her head. "Yes. It must be a surprise for me from Daddy. I am sure I am not supposed to know about it."

"Oh. My. Gosh."

"I will tell everyone about it in school tomorrow."

"Oh boy, oh boy, oh boy! I cannot wait!" cried Karen.

3

FREE COSTUMES

Hannie woke up early the next morning. "Daddy? When are you leaving for work?" she asked. "Can you drive me to school early?"

"Sure," replied her father. "Why?"

"Because of, um, because of . . ." Hannie did not want to spoil her father's surprise. "Well, just something. I need to get there early, that is all. Okay?"

"Okay."

Hannie was the very first person to arrive in her classroom that morning. The next person was Sara Ford.

"Sara! Sara!" exclaimed Hannie. "Good news!"

"Really? What is it?" asked Sara.

Hannie followed Sara into the coatroom. "My father works for a company that makes Halloween costumes, and this year he is getting free costumes for everyone in our class!"

"For *every*one?" Sara repeated. "Cool."

"Yup." Hannie glanced at the doorway and saw Tammy and Terri. "Hey, you guys, guess what. My father works for a company that makes Halloween costumes, and this year he is getting free costumes for all the kids in our class. They are really good costumes too," Hannie added.

"Wow," said Tammy.

"Excellent," said Terri.

A few minutes later Chris Lamar showed up.

"Hey, Chris!" cried Sara. "Guess what. Hannie's father works for a company that makes Halloween costumes, and he is getting *free* costumes for *all* of us this year."

"Really good costumes," said Terry.

"Truth?" Chris asked Hannie.

"Truth," replied Hannie.

The news about the costumes spread fast in Ms. Colman's room. Soon everyone was talking about Halloween.

"I was going to be a scarecrow," Natalie said to Audrey. "I was going to make my own costume. But now I guess I will wait for the really good free costume."

"I hope I can be a bat," said Audrey.

"I want to be a firefighter," said Ian.

Everyone was talking at once. Ms. Colman's room was very noisy.

Hannie waved her hands around. "Hey! Hey, everyone!" she yelled.

The kids quieted down. "What is it?" asked Karen.

"One more important thing," said Hannie. "You cannot tell Ms. Colman or your parents or anyone else about the costumes. See, my father wants to surprise me with them. And I do not want to spoil his surprise. So keep this a secret, okay?"

"Okay," said the kids.

Hannie joined Karen and Nancy in the back of the classroom.

"Hannie, this is going to be the best Halloween ever," cried Karen. "I am so glad you found out your father's secret. I cannot wait to see my costume. Isn't this cool, Nancy?"

Nancy had been staring at Hannie. Now she gave Karen a funny look. "I thought you said last Halloween was our best Halloween ever. Remember? You were

a witch, and I was your black cat?"

"I remember," said Karen. "But those were just silly costumes we made ourselves. Now Hannie is going to get us *real* costumes."

Nancy did not say anything.

"Hey, here comes Ms. Colman!" cried Bobby. "Run for your lives!"

The kids in Ms. Colman's class dashed to their desks. They were sitting quietly when Ms. Colman began the day.

"All right, girls and boys," Ms. Colman said. "You may line up by the door. And remember, only soft voices when we are in the halls, please."

It was later that morning. And it was time for the vision test.

"What is the vision test like?" Hannie whispered to Karen as they walked to the nurse's office. "Is it hard?"

"Oh, no. It is simple," Karen replied. "You just have to look at a bunch of letters and read them to the doctor. The letters get smaller and smaller. The doctor wants to see what size letter you can read. If you can only read the big ones, you might need glasses. If you can read the teeny tiny ones, then your eyes are really good."

"Oh," said Hannie. That did not sound too bad.

The nurse's office was a busy place that day. Mrs. Pazden, the school nurse, was telling everyone what to do. A teacher was writing down kids' names. An aide was helping the eye doctor. Just as Ms. Colman's class arrived, Mr. Berger's class was leaving.

"Hi, Mrs. Pazden!" called Karen. "I do not need to take the test, because I am getting glasses very soon. So I will be your helper today."

"Well . . . all right," replied Mrs. Pazden. "I did not know I was going to have another helper today. But let's see. Why don't you help Ms. Colman line up your classmates?"

Karen's classmates were already lined up. "Done!" called Karen. "That was too easy. What is next?"

Mrs. Pazden did not answer, though.

"Karen, you can help *me*," said Nancy. "I am scared."

"Scared? What are you scared of?" asked Karen.

"Glasses. I do not want them."

"Neither do I," said Hannie.

"Well, you probably do not need them."

"*You* needed them," pointed out Nancy.

"Well, that is true."

"I know!" said Hannie. "Nancy, let's not think about glasses. Let's think about our excellent Halloween costumes instead. The ones my father is going to get for us."

"Hannie — " Nancy started to say.

But Ms. Colman interrupted her. "All right, kids. Listen up, please."

It was time for the vision tests to begin.

One by one, the kids were called into a room inside the nurse's office. Hannie was the fourth to go in.

"Uh-oh," she said.

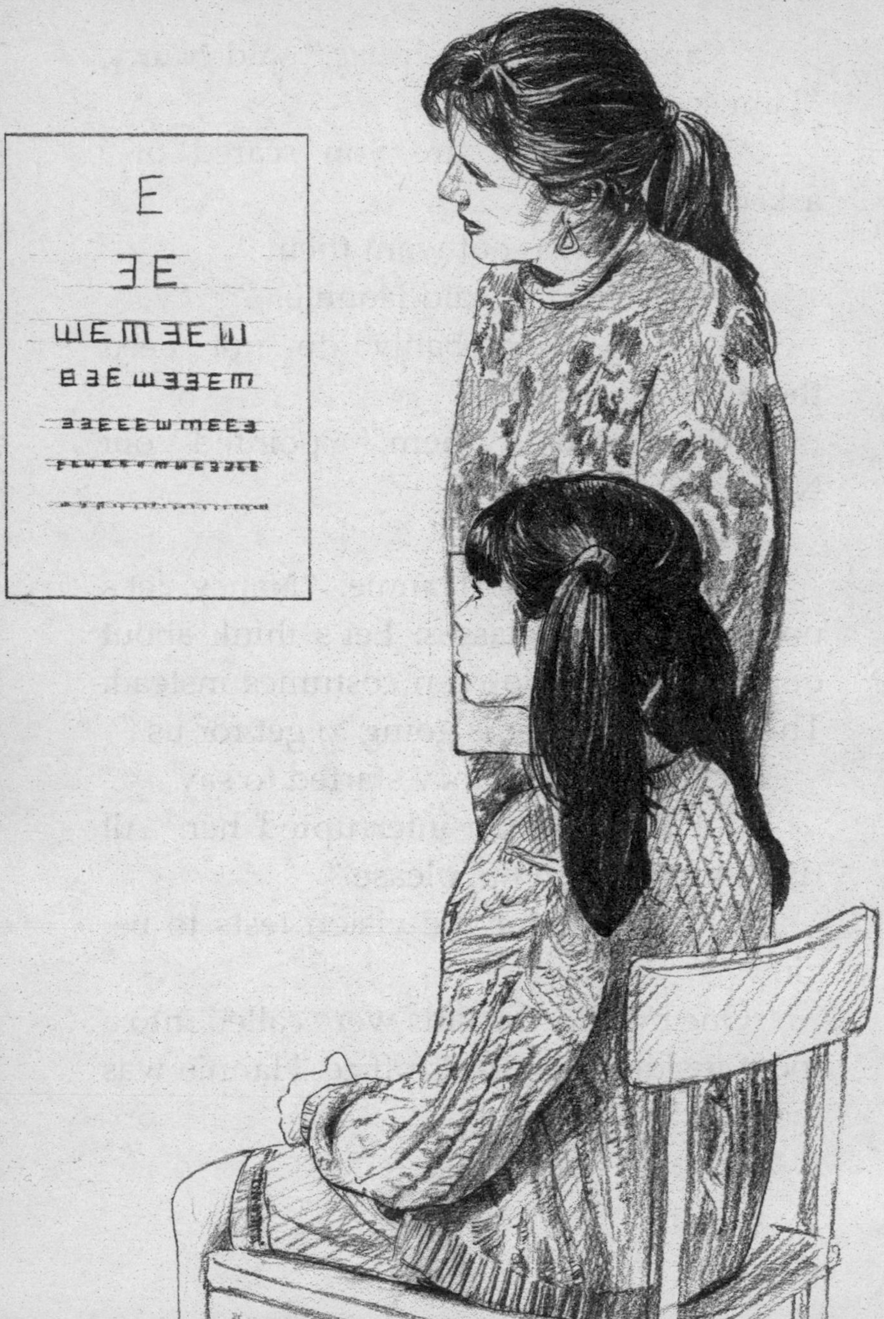

"Do not be nervous," whispered Karen.

Hannie was only nervous at first. Then she saw that Karen was right. All she had to do was say the names of letters. That was easy, easy, easy. After she had read the rows of letters (right down to the bottom), the doctor asked her to look at some big Es and tell her which way the "legs" were pointing.

"Right . . . left . . . down . . . up," said Hannie.

"That is fine," said the doctor. "Your vision is excellent. You do not need glasses. Here. Hand this paper to Mrs. Pazden on your way out."

"Yes!" exclaimed Hannie when she was standing with Karen and Nancy again. "I passed the test!"

Hannie was not the only one. The doctor told almost every kid that he or she had passed the test and did not need glasses. Natalie already had glasses, though. The doctor told her to keep wearing them. Then the doctor told Ricky that she was going to call his parents because Ricky needed to see his own eye doctor.

"Hmm," said Karen. "I wonder why."

"Hmm," said Hannie and Nancy. Then Hannie glanced at Nancy and smiled. But Nancy walked ahead of Hannie to catch up with Karen.

WINNERS

A day went by. The kids in Ms. Colman's class forgot about the vision tests. They were busy with other things. With reading stories and writing their own stories, and with cutting out pumpkins from orange paper. They made black cats and round yellow moons and ghosts and witches' brooms too.

"I cannot wait for the Halloween parade," said Hank one day.

"What Halloween parade?" asked Sara. (Sara was new in school.)

"Our school parade," Hank told her. "We have it every year."

"We bring our costumes to school on

Halloween," added Jannie. "And after lunch we change into them."

"Then everybody in the whole school goes to the gym," said Omar. "And each class gets to march around so everyone else can see their costumes. The teachers give out prizes."

"They do? What for?" asked Sara.

"Oh, for funniest costume, scariest face, stuff like that."

"Hey, I just thought of something!" cried Bobby. "With our great costumes this year, we will probably win *all* the prizes!"

"Oh, boy!" cried Karen.

The kids in Ms. Colman's class were growing very excited.

"What kinds of prizes do they give out?" asked Sara.

"Good ones," replied Tammy.

"Markers," said Leslie.

"Little toys," said Audrey.

"Once, in kindergarten, I got a coupon for a movie ticket," said Ian.

"I cannot wait!" cried Sara.

"Let's look at the calendar and see how many days are left before the Halloween parade," said Nancy.

The kids crowded around the calendar at the front of the room.

"There is Halloween," said Hannie, pointing.

"Hey, look. It is on Sunday!" exclaimed Sara. "We do not have school on Sunday. Will we still have the parade?"

"It will be on Friday," said Karen. "I heard the teachers talking."

Hannie began counting the squares on the calendar. "Eighteen days until Halloween," she announced. "And sixteen days until the parade."

"Sixteen days until we win prizes!" cried Chris.

"Hannie, thank you for getting our costumes," said Sara.

"This is going to be the best Halloween ever, thanks to Hannie," said Audrey. Audrey pulled something out of her desk. "Here, Hannie. This is for you," she added. Audrey gave Hannie a stick of gum.

"Thanks!" said Hannie.

The next day Natalie brought Hannie some stickers. "To say thank you," she said. "I am so excited about my costume!"

"This is for you too," added Omar. He gave her a baseball card. "Because I bet our class is going to win more prizes than any class has ever won. And we are only in second grade."

"Wow, thanks," said Hannie. "Thanks, you guys."

The next day Hank let Hannie cut in front of him in the lunch line. Then Jannie let Hannie have the best hopscotch court, the one that had just been painted.

"I sure am lucky," Hannie said to Nancy and Karen as they began their game. "Everyone is being so nice to me."

"Yeah!" agreed Karen.

But Nancy did not say anything. Not a word. She just tossed her stone and began the game. "Okay, Karen," she said finally. "You go next."

6

FOUR-EYES!

It was a sleepy morning. Rain was falling. Hannie looked lazily out the windows in Ms. Colman's room. She wished she could go back to bed. Instead, she was sitting at her desk by herself, waiting for her classmates to arrive. And the very next two people to arrive were Karen and Nancy. Karen was wearing . . .

"Glasses!" cried Hannie. "Karen, you got your glasses! They do not look too bad." Karen's glasses were pink.

"Not too bad?" repeated Nancy. "*I* think Karen's glasses look great."

Hannie could feel her cheeks getting hot. "Well, that is what I meant — " she

28

started to say. "Um, I mean, oh, cool! Pink glasses!"

"Do you really like them?" asked Karen.

"I really do," said Hannie.

The other kids began to trickle into Ms. Colman's room. Half of them did not even notice Karen's glasses. Tammy just said, "Oh, Karen, you got your glasses." Sara said the same thing.

Ms. Colman told Karen she liked her glasses very much. So did Natalie. (Ms. Colman and Natalie wore glasses themselves.)

Hannie and Karen and Nancy were just settling down in the back of the room when Ricky ran in. He spotted Karen right away.

"Ooh-ooh. Four-eyes!" he cried. "Hey, Karen. Are you just blind, or are you as blind as an ugly old bat?"

"You are so dumb, Ricky," Karen replied. "I am not blind at all. And anyway, what if I really *were* blind?"

29

Yeah, thought Hannie. Ricky's question was very rude.

Ricky did not answer Karen. "Blind as a bat," he said one more time, just to make her mad.

Karen stuck her tongue out at Ricky.

Then Ms. Colman clapped her hands. It was time to start the day.

All morning long Ricky would lean back in his chair, behind Hannie, and call down to Karen at the other end of the row. "Four-eyes!" he would whisper loudly. Or "Batwoman!"

Hannie and Nancy and Karen tried to ignore him.

Near the end of the day, Ms. Colman called Karen to her desk.

Uh-oh, thought Hannie. Was Karen in trouble? Hannie had passed her a mean note about Ricky. Maybe Ms. Colman had seen that. Maybe Ms. Colman was going to call Hannie to her desk next.

But that was not what happened at all.

What happened was that after Karen spoke with Ms. Colman, she tiptoed to the back of the room (she did not want to disturb her classmates during Free Reading Time) and began to take her things out of her desk.

"What are you doing?" Nancy whispered to her.

"Ms. Colman wants me to move to the front of the room. She says people who wear glasses can see better from the first row. She wants me to sit next to Natalie. In Hank's place."

"Where is Hank going to sit?" asked Hannie.

"Back here. At my desk," replied Karen.

"But — but you cannot move!" cried Nancy. "I do not want you to move, Karen! You are my best friend."

For heaven's sake, thought Hannie. Karen was not moving to a different town. Just to a different row. Hannie did not want her to move either, but why was Nancy so upset?

31

"I'm sorry. I have to move," Karen told Nancy. "Ms. Colman said so. But look. You are still sitting next to Hannie. And Hannie is my other best friend, so she should be your other best friend too."

Nancy pouted.

And Hannie realized the truth then. Nancy did not think of Hannie as her best friend. In fact, she was jealous. She was jealous of Karen's friendship with Hannie. And she was probably jealous that Hannie was getting those great costumes for everyone. Hmm. Hannie did not know what to do about Nancy.

THE COWGIRL

One morning, while Hannie and Karen and Nancy were waiting for school to begin, Karen said, "Do you guys want to come over this afternoon?"

"You mean us?" asked Hannie.

"*Both* of us?" asked Nancy.

"Sure," replied Karen. "Hannie, your mom can drive you over, can't she?"

"Well . . . I guess so."

"Goody," said Karen.

But Hannie did not feel excited. She and Karen and Nancy had not played together after school very often. And Hannie thought there might be a good reason for that. She and Karen were best friends. And

Karen and Nancy were best friends. But Hannie and Nancy — that was a different story.

Hannie went to Karen's anyway, though. When her mother dropped her off that afternoon, Hannie saw Karen and Nancy sitting together on Karen's front steps.

"Hi!" called Karen.

"Hi," Hannie replied. "What are you doing?"

"Talking about Halloween," said Karen. "Remember the year you were Paddington Bear? And your hat kept blowing off?"

Hannie giggled. "Yeah. I wonder what I will be this year."

"I cannot wait until those cool costumes come," said Karen. "I wonder what the costumes will be."

"Well, I already know what I am going to be," said Nancy.

"You do? How?" asked Hannie.

35

"Because I am making my costume myself. That will be much more fun. Besides, I do not want some costume I have never seen before. I want to choose it myself. And I want to be a cowgirl. I already have the hat and boots. And my mom and I are making a vest with fringe on it."

Hannie's tummy felt a little funny. "So you do not want one of the costumes my father is getting?" she asked.

"No. Thank you. I do not need one," replied Nancy.

"Oh," said Hannie.

Hannie could not stop thinking about what Nancy had said. She thought about it for the rest of the afternoon. When her father picked her up on his way home from work, Hannie was in a very bad mood.

THE BIG MISTAKE

The days passed. The kids in Ms. Colman's class looked at the big calendar every day. They were counting down to the Halloween parade.

On Tuesday, three days before the parade, Ricky said, "Hannie, have our costumes come yet?"

"No, but they will be here in time for Halloween."

"Will they be here in time for the parade?"

"Oh, of course," replied Hannie.

But the costumes did not arrive that afternoon. Hannie thought about asking her father about them that night, but she did not want to spoil his surprise. By the next day, though, her classmates were nervous.

"Where are they, Hannie?" asked Natalie.

"The parade is in *two days*," added Leslie.

"We need to try the costumes on," said Sara. "What if they do not fit?"

"Well," said Hannie, "I am *sure* my father is going to bring them home tonight."

And if he does not, Hannie said to herself, I will ask him about them.

When Hannie's father returned from work that night, Hannie pounced on him.

"Hi, Daddy!" she cried. She looked around. She did not see any costumes. So she had to ask, "Where are the costumes, Daddy?"

"What costumes?" said Mr. Papadakis.

"Oh, Daddy. I already know about the surprise. And I am sorry to spoil it. But it was a very good surprise. So now you can show me the costumes." Mr. Papadakis

was frowning. "The Halloween costumes," Hannie went on. "I heard you talking about them on the phone. You said everything was ordered and would be here in time for Halloween. And that there would be plenty for everyone. So then I knew. You got free costumes for all my classmates — "

"Whoa, Hannie. Slow down," said her father gently. "I think you misunderstood something. I was not talking about costumes. I was talking about a Halloween party at our office. I am in charge of it. I had to order the food and decorations. And I managed to get free party favors for everyone."

"So you did not get costumes for my friends and me?"

"Well . . . no. I did not know anything about that."

That funny feeling had crept into Hannie's tummy again. "Um, then *can* you get us free costumes? I mean, your company makes costumes, doesn't it?"

"Yes, but Hannie, the costumes are in

stores by now. And the extras are in our warehouse — and the warehouse is in Illinois."

"Illinois?" Hannie was not sure where that was, but it sounded far away from Connecticut.

"Yes. And Hannie, I cannot just get free things from the company whenever I want. I would have to make special arrangements. And *sixteen* free costumes would be a very big deal."

"Oh."

Hannie did not know what to say. So she went to her room. She lay on her bed. She covered her head with her pillow. Hannie knew she was in big, big trouble. The next day was Thursday, the day before the Halloween parade. Her friends *might* have time to buy or make costumes before Sunday for trick-or-treating. But they would probably not have time to get costumes for the parade. What were her classmates going to do? They were excited about the parade. They had told everyone they were going to win all the prizes.

And now Hannie was going to let them down. Every single one. Hannie began to cry.

SQUARE-EYES

Hannie did not sleep well that night. She woke up a lot. And every time she woke up, she thought about the costumes. She knew there was only one thing she could do the next morning. She would have to give her classmates the bad news.

Hannie was the fourth person to arrive in her class the next day. Leslie, Jannie, and Chris were already there.

"Hannie!" Leslie cried. "Where are—"

Then Leslie stopped speaking. She was looking at something behind Hannie. Hannie turned around. Ricky was entering the room. And he was wearing . . . glasses.

44

Ricky looked as if he wanted to hide behind Hannie.

"Hey! Are those *glasses*?" cried Chris.

Ricky hurried to his desk. "Yes," he muttered.

A few more kids came into the room. They spotted Ricky right away. When Karen spotted him, she looked cross. "Ricky, are you imitating me? Are you making fun of me?" she asked. "My glasses are not *that* bad," she said, looking at the big square glasses perched on Ricky's nose. Then she stopped. "Very funny, Ricky. Okay, you can take them off now. . . ." Karen's voice trailed away. Ricky's lip was trembling. "Ricky? What is wrong?" asked Karen.

"They are real glasses," Ricky whispered. "They are not a joke. I had to get them, just like you."

The kids crowded around Ricky's desk.

"Four-eyes!" said Hank.

"Bat*man*!" cried Omar.

"Square-eyes!" called Hannie. She could not help herself.

"Boys and girls, what is going on in here?" asked Ms. Colman. She stood at her desk while the kids ran to their seats.

"Ricky got glasses!" Audrey called gleefully.

"My goodness. Another glasses-wearer," said Ms. Colman. "Ricky, you look very handsome." (Hannie snorted.) "All right. It is time to change some seats again. Ricky, you need to move to the front row with Natalie and Karen."

"Ew," said Karen. (She said it quietly.)

"Let me see," Ms. Colman went on. "Ricky and Jannie, why don't the two of you trade places. Jannie, you move to the back next to Hannie. And Ricky, you move to the front next to Karen."

Hannie was not sorry to see Ricky move. He was a tease. And he had been bothering her since the beginning of second grade. But she was not sure how she felt about Jannie, since Jannie and Leslie did not like Hannie or Karen or Nancy very much.

Hannie wanted to lean over and whisper to Nancy that Meanie-mo Jannie was moving in. But right now, Nancy did not like Hannie very much either. Hannie sighed loudly.

Ricky and Jannie emptied out their desks. A lot of junk fell out of Ricky's — scraps of paper, parts of erasers, lint from his pockets, bitten-off sticks of chewing gum. It took him a long time to clean out his stuff, and a long time to carry his things to the front of the room. But at last he was gone, and Jannie was sitting next to Hannie.

Jannie grinned at Hannie. "Where are our costumes?" she asked. "Is your father bringing them over later or something?"

Hannie's stomach flip-flopped. She had almost forgotten about the costumes. Now she would have to tell the truth.

"Well," Hannie began, "the thing is, um, I was wrong. I made a mistake. My father did not get us costumes after all."

"He did not get costumes?" cried Jannie. "What are we going to do? The parade is tomorrow! Hannie, you are —"

"Okay, kids. It is time to settle down," said Ms. Colman. "Quiet, please."

The kids quieted down. But Jannie turned to Hannie and whispered, "You have ruined Halloween, Hannie Papadakis."

NANCY'S GOOD IDEA

Hannie felt horrible. She had ruined Halloween. A whole *holiday*. It was the worst thing she had ever done.

By recess every kid in Ms. Colman's class knew about the costumes. That was because Jannie had told Leslie, Leslie had told the twins, Terri had told Natalie and Ian, and Tammy had told Omar and Audrey. That was before lunch. During lunch, the rest of the kids found out.

And after lunch, the kids surrounded Hannie on the playground.

"What are we going to do about costumes?" Leslie said to Hannie.

"Well . . . today is only Thursday. Halloween is on Sunday," said Hannie. "You have three days to get costumes. Or make them."

"Hannie, have you looked in the stores?" asked Ricky. "There is nothing left. Just old stuff no one wants. Like broken fangs. And bent witches' hats."

"Dirty costumes from last year," added Sara.

"And besides, the parade is *tomorrow*," added Chris. "Not in three days. If we want to be in the parade, we need costumes in *one* day. You ruined the parade, Hannie."

"Yeah, now we will not win any prizes," added Tammy.

A holiday ruiner and a parade ruiner. Hannie's lip began to tremble.

"You guys," said Karen. She stepped through the crowd of kids. She stood next to Hannie. "You guys leave Hannie alone. She did not do anything wrong."

"Yes she did. She wrecked Halloween because she is so stupid," said Leslie.

"She is not stupid!" cried Karen. "She just made a mistake."

"What do you know, Four-eyes?" called Bobby.

"Oh, Bobby. Get a life," replied Karen. "Quit picking on everyone."

"Square-eyes!" called Bobby anyway.

"Well, I know one person who can be in the parade," grumbled Hannie. "Nancy. She made her own costume."

Hannie glared at Nancy. To her surprise, Nancy did not glare back. Instead, she

smiled. Then she stepped forward. She stood on the other side of Hannie. "Maybe I did," said Nancy, "but I am not going to march in the parade all by myself. Besides, I think you guys are being very mean to Hannie. It is not nice to call people names. It is not nice to tease them about glasses or about anything else. Anyway, I think *glasses* would make good costumes for the parade."

"Thanks a lot, Nancy," said Karen.

"Not your glasses, Karen. Most people hardly notice regular old glasses. *Most* people," she went on, glaring at Bobby. "No, I mean the funny kind with the nose and mustache attached. What if we all wore them in the parade tomorrow?"

The kids were quiet for a moment. Then Audrey said, "Glasses are not really costumes."

"But they *would* look kind of funny," said Ian. "I mean, if we were all wearing them. Maybe Ms. Colman would wear them too."

"Let's talk to her after recess," said Karen.

When recess was over, Hannie, Nancy, and Karen hurried to their classroom.

"Ms. Colman, we have to talk to you!" cried Karen.

"What is it?" asked Ms. Colman.

Karen and Nancy looked at Hannie. Then Hannie told her teacher the long, sad story about the Halloween costumes. After that, Nancy told her about her glasses idea.

"Hmm," said Ms. Colman. "I think we can get seventeen pairs of funny glasses. I know where to buy them. And we can pay for them out of our class account. Are you sure that is what you kids want to do?"

"We are sure," replied Hannie and her friends.

THE COSTUME
PARTY

After school that day, Hannie said to Nancy, "You know, you could wear your costume in the parade tomorrow. You should let everyone see it. You should not waste it."

"No," replied Nancy. "I do not want to be the only one in our class with a whole costume. Besides, I want to stick with you guys."

"Thanks, Nancy," said Hannie.

Hannie was glad about the glasses. Now her classmates could be in the parade. And the other kids would probably think the glasses were funny. Still, Hannie knew she had let her friends down. She had promised them fantastic costumes. And she had gotten them . . . nothing.

After supper that night, Hannie told her parents about the glasses. And about what had happened on the playground.

"Nancy came to your rescue, didn't she?" said Mrs. Papadakis.

"Yes," said Hannie. "I did not think she would do that."

"It sounds as if she really wants to be your friend."

"I guess so. That would be nice. I would be very happy if Karen and Nancy and I were all best friends."

Mr. Papadakis had been looking thoughtful. "You know, Hannie," he said finally, "a few years ago, we cleaned out our offices and I brought home several cartons of costume parts. I had forgotten about that until now. The boxes are sitting out in the garage. They are full of eye patches, wigs, masks — "

"In the garage?" interrupted Hannie. "I want to go look at them!"

Hannie ran into the garage. Her father followed her. "They are over here," he said. He led Hannie to five large cartons stacked against a wall. He opened two of them.

"Oh! Oh, excellent!" exclaimed Hannie. "Look! Masks and wigs and rubber hands. And eye patches, just like you said. And here are hats. Oh, and fabric and sequins and feathers and all kinds of stuff. We could make great costumes! Daddy?"

"Yes?"

"I have an idea. It is too late for the parade. But my friends and I could use these things to make costumes for trick-or-treating. Could I invite my classmates to come over on Saturday? We could have a costume-making party."

"Well . . . sure," said Mr. Papadakis. "If your mother says yes."

Mrs. Papadakis said yes too.

Hannie could not wait to tell her friends the good news.

12

THE PARADE

The next morning, Hannie bounced into her classroom. Lots of other kids had already arrived, and Hannie was glad.

"Attention, please! Attention! I have an announcement to make," said Hannie. Hannie stood on her chair to make herself tall. Standing on chairs was not really allowed. But Hannie felt that this was an important occasion. Plus, Ms. Colman had not arrived yet.

The kids gathered around Hannie.

"You are all invited to a costume party at my house tomorrow," said Hannie. "I hope you can come."

"A costume party? But we do not have costumes," said Terri.

"Thanks to Hannie," Bobby muttered.

"This is a costume-*making* party," said Hannie. She told her friends about the boxes in the garage.

"*I* can come!" cried Karen.

"Me too!" said Natalie.

A few kids said they needed to ask their parents about the party. But in the end, every one of them seemed excited.

"We will have Halloween costumes after all!" exclaimed Audrey.

"Real ones," Sara added.

Hannie felt quite a bit better.

After recess that day Ms. Colman said, "It is almost time for the Halloween parade. I am sorry about your costumes. But at least we have our seventeen pairs of funny glasses." Ms. Colman reached under her desk and pulled out a carton. She opened it. Then she held up a pair of thick black glasses. Over the glasses were fuzzy black eyebrows. Under the glasses was a large nose, and under the nose was a fuzzy black mustache.

"Cool!" said Ricky. He began to laugh.

"Yeah, those are funny!" exclaimed Bobby.

"Yeah, *those* are funny," said Karen sternly. "But Ricky's glasses and Natalie's glasses and my glasses are just regular. Not funny. Right, Bobby?"

"Um, right," agreed Bobby.

"Well, let's put our glasses on and go to the gym," said Ms. Colman.

When Hannie and her classmates reached the gym, Hannie looked around at the other kids. She saw monsters and princesses and ghosts. She saw the Cat in the Hat and Snow White and a car. She even saw a bunch of grapes.

"Everyone has really good costumes," Hannie whispered to Nancy.

"So will we, after tomorrow," Nancy replied. "Besides, I like our glasses. They are pretty funny. Look at Ms. Colman."

Hannie looked at her teacher and started to giggle.

The parade began. Class by class, the kids showed off their costumes to the rest of the students and the teachers.

"And now for Ms. Colman's class," Mrs. Titus, the principal, said finally.

Hannie's stomach began to jump and flutter. But she stood up with her class-mates, and they walked around the gym.

Sixteen kids and their teacher with the same goofy face. The other students began to laugh. Some of the teachers clapped.

"They like us!" Hannie whispered to Karen and Nancy.

And they did. Later, when Mrs. Titus announced the winners of the prizes, she called out, "And for silliest costume — the kids in Ms. Colman's class." She handed Hannie and each of her classmates (and even Ms. Colman) a Halloween pencil.

Hannie grinned. She had not ruined Halloween after all.

13

GOBLINS AND
PIRATES AND CLOWNS

On Saturday morning Mr. Papadakis said, "Are you ready to be a pastry chef, Hannie?" He handed her an apron.

"I am all ready," replied Hannie.

Hannie and her father were going to make cupcakes for the costume party. Hannie knew her friends would not have time to do much at the party except make their costumes. But she at least wanted to serve them a special treat. She and her parents had decided on cider and cupcakes. Hannie and her dad were going to frost the cupcakes with orange icing and make faces on them with black jellybeans.

"Just like jack-o'-lanterns," said Hannie.

By two o'clock that afternoon, Hannie was ready for her party.

At 2:01 the doorbell rang. Karen and Nancy were the first to arrive.

"Nancy, you already have a costume!" said Hannie.

"I know. But I did not want to miss the party. I will just help everyone else make their costumes."

"So will I," said the next guest.

"Ms. Colman! You came too!" cried Hannie. "Goody!"

"Where is all the costume stuff?" asked Karen.

"In the garage," replied Hannie. "And that is where we are going to have our party, since it is not too cold today. But let's wait until everyone else gets here."

Hannie and her friends did not have to

wait long. The kids in their class arrived in groups. Before they knew it, every single guest had shown up.

"Okay, it is time to go to the garage," said Hannie.

That morning Hannie's parents had parked their cars in the street. They had set up two long tables in the garage. On one table they had piled the wigs and other costume parts. On the other table they had set out the fabric and feathers and sequins, along with glue and scissors.

"Okay, kids, go to work," said Mr. Papadakis. "And have fun."

"Don't worry about making a mess," added Mrs. Papadakis. "The garage is already a mess."

The kids set to work.

"What are you going to be, Hannie?" asked Nancy.

Hannie looked thoughtful. "I was going to be a magic genie. But now I want to be something different."

"How about a mouse?" suggested Nancy.

"A *mouse*?" said Hannie. "A mouse. Hmmm. Well . . ."

"We could use gray and pink felt to make mouse ears for you. Maybe we could make you little paws or something too."

"Okay. Cool!" said Hannie.

Hannie and Nancy set to work. Around them their classmates were laughing and talking. And cutting and gluing and folding and measuring and thinking.

Sara was gluing feathers onto cardboard to make flapping bird's wings. Bobby had collected a mask and an eye patch for a pirate's costume. Chris was saying, "What could I use to make a cat's tail?" Ms. Colman bustled around and helped anyone who needed help.

"Karen, what kind of costume are you making?" asked Hannie.

"It is a secret," Karen replied. "But you will find out soon."

Hannie looked at the things Karen had

collected. "Are you an old lady? A witch again?" she guessed.

Karen zipped her lip.

"This is fun, isn't it?" said Audrey.

"Yes," agreed Hannie. "Much more fun than getting ready-made costumes."

MOTHER GOOSE

Two hours later the parents started to arrive. It was time for the costume party to end.

"Look at me! I am a parrot!" exclaimed Sara.

"I am a bee," said Terri.

"I am a goblin," said Ricky.

"With glasses?" asked Bobby. He snorted.

"Bobby, have you ever seen a goblin?" said Ricky.

"Of course not," replied Bobby.

"Then how do you know they do not wear glasses?"

"Ha!" cried Karen. "Good one, Ricky!"

The kids laughed. (Bobby scowled.)

"Bobby," said Ms. Colman gently, "perhaps you do not need to mention glasses anymore."

"They really are not all that interesting," added Chris. "They are just glasses. Ms. Colman wears them. My mother wears them."

"My father wears them," said Omar.

"My grandma and grandpa wear them," said Hank. "And my cousin. Well, three of my cousins. And my — "

"Okay, okay!" cried Bobby.

Hannie looked at Karen and Nancy. The girls smiled at each other. Hannie knew the teasing was over.

"Good-bye, Hannie!" called the kids as they left the garage. "Thanks! Thanks for the cupcakes too!"

"Good-bye! Happy Halloween!" Hannie called back.

At last only Karen and Nancy were left.

"I am staying at my dad's this week-

end," said Karen. "So I can go home whenever I want."

"My dad is not going to pick me up until later," said Nancy. "He said I could play at Karen's after the party."

"Play here instead," said Hannie. "At least for a little while."

The girls helped Hannie's parents clean up the garage. Then Hannie said, "Karen, will you show us your costume now?"

Karen grinned. "Okay. Let me go put it on." Karen ran into the garage. "You guys stay outside," she called. "I will be there in a minute."

When Karen stepped outside, she was wearing a hood covered with white feathers. She was wearing white-feathered wings too, and pants covered in white feathers. A pink shawl was wrapped around her shoulders. Instead of a mask, she was wearing an orange beak. Above the beak were perched her glasses.

"Guess who I am," said Karen.

Hannie paused. "Who?"

"Mother Goose!"

"Oh! Excellent!" cried Nancy.

"And your glasses are part of the costume," said Hannie.

"Yup. Mother Goose wears glasses. At least she does in a book I checked out of the library last weekend."

"Hannie? Where is your costume?" asked Nancy.

"Inside. I am going to be the best mouse." Hannie thought of her pink ears, her mouse mask with the whiskers, and her mouse paws. "I will wear everything with my gray leotard and gray tights."

"Can we see?" asked Karen. "I want to see it all put together."

"Well . . . I was thinking you could see it tomorrow. I was wondering if you — both of you — wanted to trick-or-treat with me."

"Trick-or-treat together? All three of us?" asked Nancy. "Now that is a wonderful, Halloweeny idea!"

THE SPOOKY NIGHT

"Hannie, are you ready?"

Hannie had run into her kitchen to answer the telephone. The caller had not said, "Hello" or "How are you?" or even her name. She had just said, "Hannie, are you ready?"

But Hannie knew who was on the phone. It was Karen. And she wanted to go trick-or-treating.

"Almost ready," Hannie replied. "But Karen, it is not even dark outside yet. Don't you want to wait until dark?"

"I guess. Nancy is already here, though. And . . . it is hard to wait!"

"Well, why don't you come over in half an hour, okay?"

"Okay." Karen sighed and hung up the phone.

Hannie was already wearing her gray leotard and tights. She was wearing them over long underwear. Even so, her mother had said she would have to wear a coat over her costume.

"Mice do not wear coats!" Hannie had said.

"That is because they have fur," her mother had replied. "But you are a girl. And you do not have fur. Thank goodness," she added. "So I am afraid you must wear a coat."

In the end, Hannie was allowed to wear an old *gray* coat of Linny's, so that was not so bad.

When the bell rang half an hour later, Hannie was ready for trick-or-treating. She ran to the door in her mouse outfit and the gray coat. She was carrying a large goody bag.

Standing at the door were Karen in her Mother Goose costume, Nancy in her cowgirl costume, and Kristy. Kristy was Karen's big stepsister, and an excellent baby-sitter. She had said she would be happy to take Hannie and Nancy and Karen trick-or-treating.

"Let's go! Let's go!" cried Karen, jumping up and down.

"Wait. We have to look at Hannie's costume," said Nancy. "Stand back, Hannie."

Hannie stood back. She opened her coat.

"Cool," said Nancy.

"Great. Okay, let's go," said Karen.

Hannie and Nancy and Karen took one another's hands. They ran outside. They ran next door. Kristy was right behind them.

"Ooh, spooky," said Hannie as the girls reached the house next door.

A line of glowing jack-o'-lanterns lit the path to the front porch. A ghost was hanging by the door. Two more ghosts hung from the branches of a tree nearby.

When Hannie rang the bell, instead of a dingdong, she heard a long, low moan, and then a cackle.

"Yipes!" Nancy squeezed Hannie's hand.

Slowly the door to the house creaked open.

"Heh, heh, heh." A monster answered the door.

Hannie paused. She glanced at Karen and Nancy. Finally Karen said, "Um, trick-or-treat?"

"I will give you a treat, I guess," said the monster. "You are wearing such lovely costumes. Let me see. What *kind* of a treat shall I give you?" Hannie was about to suggest a Snickers bar when the monster said, "An ox knuckle? Or some hair from a hyena?"

"No!" shrieked the girls.

"Oh." The monster sounded disappointed. "Then how about some Reese's Pieces?"

"Yes!" cried the girls.

The monster gave a bag of candy to Hannie, to Nancy, and then to Karen.

"Thank you!" called the girls.

"Ooh, that was spooky," Hannie whispered to Nancy.

"But fun," Nancy whispered back.

"Let's go to the next house!" said Karen.

The girls ran off in their costumes. Trick-or-treating had just begun.

About the Author

ANN M. MARTIN lives in New York City and loves animals, especially cats. She has two cats of her own, Gussie and Woody.

Other books by Ann M. Martin that you might enjoy are *Stage Fright*; *Me and Katie (the Pest)*; and the books in *The Baby-sitters Club* series.

Ann likes ice cream and *I Love Lucy*. And she has her own little sister, whose name is Jane.

THE KIDS IN MS. COLMAN'S CLASS

Don't miss #10
HOLIDAY TIME

"Soon it will be December," said Ms. Colman, once she had taken attendance. "December is when three important holidays take place. Does everyone know what they are?"

"Christmas!" Karen shouted.

Sara raised her hand. "Kwanzaa," she said.

"That is right," said Ms. Colman. "And one more."

"Hanukkah," said Nancy.

"Very good," said Ms. Colman. "Hanukkah, Kwanzaa, and Christmas are three important holidays. Today we are starting a new unit about those three holidays."

Meet some new friends!

THE KIDS IN Ms. COLMAN'S CLASS

by Ann M. Martin

There's always something going on in Ms. Colman's class!
Read about the adventures of Baby-sitters Little Sister Karen
Brewer...and everyone else in the second grade.